Series 561

When three little ships sailed from Palos in 1492 they changed the course of history. This is the story of the man who commanded them, Christopher Columbus, and of the most momentous voyage ever made by man.

Christopher Columbus

by L DU GARDE PEACH OBE MA PhD DLitt
with illustrations by JOHN KENNEY

Ladybird Books Loughborough

CHRISTOPHER COLUMBUS

When Christopher Columbus sailed from the little port of Palos, in Spain, on August the third, in the year 1492, he commenced a voyage which changed the course of history.

This is the story of what is perhaps one of the most important events in the long history of mankind.

Christopher Columbus was born in Genoa, in Italy, between the years 1440 and 1450, although the exact date is not known. Genoa is a seaport, and Columbus must have spent much of his time down in the harbour, watching the ships come and go, and talking with the sailors.

The ships of those days were, of course, sailing ships, and very much smaller than the steamships of to-day. They were gaily painted, with coloured sails and high sterns, sometimes with battlements round them like a castle on land.

It was in a ship of this kind that Columbus was to sail on his great voyage of discovery, forty years later.

We know very little about the early life of Columbus. In a book written by his son, we read that he was a student at the University of Pavia, but Columbus himself stated that when he was fourteen years old he was a sailor.

He probably was a sailor at that age, because in those days young men did many things before they settled down to a trade. His father was a weaver, and for a time Christopher certainly worked in the family business.

We do not know what made him leave it, but the mystery of the sea must always have had a fascination for him. In those days men knew nothing of the open sea beyond a few miles from the shore.

The voyages made by Columbus took him down the west coast of Africa, where he was very nearly captured by pirates, and northward up the coasts of Spain and France. He visited England, and probably sailed as far north as Iceland.

About the year 1479 Columbus went to live on the island of Porto Santo, which you will find on the map, close to Madeira. This island was owned by Portugal.

Here many things happened which were to help Columbus in making up his mind to explore the unknown ocean to the west.

The first of these was his marriage to the daughter of a man named Bartholomew Perestrello, a sea captain and a famous navigator. By his father-in-law, Columbus was given charts and navigating instruments, and from him he learnt all that was then known about the winds and ocean currents to the west of Madeira.

During this time Columbus earned his living by making and copying maps and charts. These were, of course, very incomplete, because North and South America were not on them at all.

Nobody knew what lay between the island of Porto Santo and Japan, and as Columbus drew his charts and gazed out over the ocean, he was filled with the desire to find out.

Columbus knew, or at least believed that the earth was round. Nobody knew this for certain, because no one had ever travelled right round it; but Columbus thought that by sailing straight to the west he would come to Japan, which other explorers had reached by journeying across land and sea to the east.

No one had any idea that there was a great continent in between. But people knew that there must be some land to the west, because of strange things which were blown on to the shores of Madeira and Porto Santo by the west wind.

Columbus spent much of his time talking to sailors down in the harbour. Here he was shown strange pieces of carved wood and huge canes, each section of which would hold a gallon of water.

No one had ever seen such things before, so they must have come from unknown lands across the sea.

Columbus determined to sail to the west in search of them. But he was a poor man, and it would first be necessary to find someone who would provide him with a ship.

He applied to King John of Portugal. The King listened carefully to what Columbus had to say, but refused to help him. Then without telling Columbus, he sent a ship manned by his own sailors to find and claim the rich land of which Columbus had spoken.

This was a very mean thing to do, but the King of Portugal gained nothing by it. After a few days at sea the sailors lost heart and returned.

When Columbus heard how the King had deceived him, he left Portugal and went to Spain.

It was not easy for a poor man to get an audience with the King and Queen of Spain. For two years Columbus waited. At last he was received at the court and hoped that his search for a ship was at an end.

He was wrong. The King of Spain was at the time engaged in fighting a war with the Moors who had occupied the country. Although he received Columbus kindly, all he would do was to form a Committee to advise him as to whether to help Columbus or not.

This Committee was composed of Spanish noblemen and priests, and for days and weeks Columbus argued and pleaded with them, moving from place to place as the Court travelled from one part of Spain to another.

The Committee was in no hurry. Some of its members refused even to believe that the earth could possibly be round. Others suggested that if the earth was round, Columbus would be sailing down hill, and as it was impossible for a ship to sail up hill, he would never get back.

It was four long years before the Committee made up its mind. It then reported to the King that the voyage proposed by Columbus was "vain and impracticable".

Columbus was not idle during those four years. He must have seen how things were going, and he decided to explore the possibility of getting a ship elsewhere.

The King of Portugal had refused to help him: the Committee of the King of Spain was putting every difficulty in his way. But Spain and Portugal were not the only countries with ships and hardy sailors.

Columbus had a brother named Bartholomew, and it was decided between them that whilst Christopher remained in Spain to argue with the Committee, Bartholomew should seek help in England.

Henry VII, the first of the Tudor Kings of England, had been on the throne for three years. He was a cautious man, careful of money, and although he received Bartholomew and listened to him patiently, he refused to find ships for a voyage which offered so uncertain a reward.

If Henry VII had been less cautious, South America might have been colonized by England.

Bartholomew reported his failure to Columbus and crossed over to France to ask for help from Charles VIII. He was again refused.

In Spain, Columbus himself was in despair. A second Committee set up by the King had endorsed the refusal of the first. It was now the year 1491.

Believing that there was no hope of help in Spain, Columbus set out to join his brother in France. On the way he rested at a monastery near Palos, where he had been kindly received some years before. This stay at the monastery of La Rabida proved to be the turning point of his fortunes.

At this monastery there was a friar named Juan Perez, who had been chaplain to the Queen of Spain. He had faith in Columbus and agreed to write to the Queen and ask for her help.

The result was beyond anything Columbus could have expected. The Queen sent a sum of money to Columbus, instructing him to buy suitable clothes and a horse, and come at once to see her.

There were to be no more Committees.

Queen Isabella received Columbus alone, and showed a lively interest in his plans. So much so, that he was again received in full Court and everything suddenly appeared to be going in his favour.

Columbus was promised ships for his venture. Then, with all the resentment of his seven years wait surging up within him, he demanded rewards far beyond anything which the King and Queen considered reasonable. Amongst these was the demand that he should at once be promoted to the rank of admiral, and be given one tenth of all the wealth to come from any new lands he might find.

His terms were refused, and immediately he set out once more to join his brother in France. Scarcely had he gone six miles when a messenger overtook him. His demands had been granted.

Columbus turned his horse's head again towards the Court. Everything was now set for the voyage which, of all those undertaken by any man, was to have the most far-reaching results.

Columbus was now assured of getting the ships he required, but actually they cost the King and Queen of Spain nothing.

The port of Palos had fallen under royal displeasure on account of unpaid taxes and many of its inhabitants were liable for heavy fines. It was a custom in Spain at that time to inflict punishment in such circumstances on a whole town, and not on individuals. Palos was therefore ordered to provide Columbus with three ships and the men to man them, at the cost of the town.

Palos was a long way from the Court, and a town which had refused to pay taxes was equally ready to refuse to obey the order to find ships. Columbus pleaded and raged in vain. When he produced the parchment with the King's commands, the men of Palos laughed at him.

Although the harbour was full of ships, none was, they said, available for such a mad voyage into nowhere.

In spite of all the difficulties he had overcome, and the long years he had waited, Columbus seemed as far from the fulfilment of his desire as ever.

When Columbus's hopes seemed to be at their lowest, fortune favoured him.

In Palos he had made the acquaintance of two brothers, sea captains, and what was more important, the owners of ships. Their names were Martin Alonso Pinzon and Vicente Yañez Pinzon.

With their help he finally obtained three small ships. Their names were 'Santa Maria', the largest of the three, 'Pinta', and 'Niña'. These were to become three of the most famous ships in the annals of the sea.

They were very small. The deck of the 'Santa Maria' was not much longer than a cricket pitch, about seventy feet. The 'Pinta' was only half the size of the 'Santa Maria', and the 'Niña' was smaller still, with a crew of only 18 men.

With these tiny ships Columbus was proposing to sail into stormy, uncharted seas, where no man had ever been, and from which few expected that he would ever return. It is not surprising that having at last got the ships, he found it difficult to persuade men to sail in them.

It would have been quite impossible if it had not been for the help of the two brothers Pinzon. They encouraged the reluctant sailors of Palos not only with words, but by their example. Both proposed to sail westwards into the unknown with Columbus.

Columbus was prepared to recruit his crews from amongst the criminals in the prisons of Spain, and he procured from the King a promise of a free pardon for any who sailed with him. Fortunately this was not necessary.

Even so, it was not easy to get together the crews, about 90 men in all, necessary to man the three ships. It was an age when people, not only in Spain, but everywhere, were deeply religious, and many thought that it was wicked to venture into the unknown. Others were afraid of the perils which their imaginations invented, great sea monsters and mysterious whirlpools in the ocean.

It was the hope of rich rewards which finally overcame fears, together with the confident example of the two most respected sea captains in the town.

Soon everything was ready. The three ships had taken aboard food and stores to last a year.

The allowance for each sailor in those days was a pound of biscuits, four pints of wine, and two-thirds of a pound of meat a day. We read that, in addition, the ships were stocked with "onions and cheese, not forgetting oil and vinegar, which are things very necessary at sea".

When we add the ships stores of sails and rope, and the stone cannon balls for the guns with which the ships were armed, it is clear that these little vessels were loaded well down to the water line.

One thing remained to be done. All felt that in voyaging into the unknown they were in the hands of God. Before sailing, Columbus and his crews, accompanied by all the men and women of Palos, went in solemn procession to the church in the monastery at La Rabida to ask God's blessing upon their enterprise.

It was here that Columbus had received the message from the Queen, and it was now the good friar, Juan Perez, who had written to her on his behalf, who blessed Columbus and his men.

It was on Friday, August the third, in the year 1492, half-an-hour before sunrise, that Columbus gave the order to cast off.

As the light grew, the sails filled, and the three little ships drew away from the quayside. One of the most momentous voyages in history had begun.

Aboard the ships the sailors were too busy sheeting home the sails and coiling the ropes to give much heed to the crowds gathered round the harbour. Wives and mothers were weeping and praying, and men were taking what they feared would be their last look at the ships' company. For this was no ordinary voyage from one coastal port to another. All looked on the crews of the 'Santa Maria', the 'Pinta', and the 'Niña', as we should look on the first space travellers setting out to the moon. Even more so, for at least we know that the moon is there.

One man alone was confident and happy as the sails caught the red light of dawn and the ships lifted to the swell coming in from the unknown seas. Christopher Columbus was his own master at last: no one could stop him now.

When he sailed from Palos, Columbus may well have thought that his troubles were at an end. Not for the first time, he was wrong.

For three days all went well. Course was set for the Canary Islands, the most westerly land known, whence Columbus proposed to take his departure. The 'Pinta', the fastest of the three, was well ahead, her white sails rising and falling against the blue-grey horizon.

Then suddenly Columbus paused as he walked the deck of the 'Santa Maria'. Something was wrong with the 'Pinta'. Her sails had been taken in and she was lying in the trough of the waves without steerage way. Soon the 'Santa Maria' was alongside, and Columbus learned that part of the rudder had been carried away and that some time would be required to repair it.

Columbus was much troubled, not by the mishap to the rudder of the 'Pinta', but by the thought that it might have been caused intentionally by members of the crew whose courage had failed them, and who hoped by damaging the rudder, to make it necessary for the 'Pinta' to return to Palos.

The attempt, if it had been intentionally made, failed. Columbus had overcome too many difficulties to be diverted from his purpose by a damaged rudder.

The voyage was resumed to Madeira and the Canaries, where a whole month was spent repairing the 'Pinta' and altering the sail plan of the 'Niña'. It was not until September the sixth that the great mainsail of the 'Santa Maria', with its large red cross emblazoned upon it, was again sheeted home for the voyage to the west.

We are fortunate in possessing Columbus's log of the voyage; that is, the day to day account of happenings always kept aboard every ship that sails the seas. For a week good progress was made, and each day by observing the sun and the stars, Columbus marked the ship's position on his chart and reckoned the distance travelled.

It was now that he began to keep two logs. In one he recorded the true number of leagues covered each day; in the other, which he showed to the crew, he entered a lesser number. He did not want the sailors to know how far they were from Spain lest they should become fearful and wish to return.

Columbus had noticed, seven days after leaving the Canaries, that the ship's compass was behaving strangely. Instead of pointing to the north star the needle had moved a little towards the north-west. He said nothing of this to the crew, but each day the needle was a little further away.

By September the seventeenth the needle had moved so far from its normal position that it was noticed by the helmsman. At once the sailors gathered round the compass, and in the words of Columbus, written in the log, they were "terrified and dismayed".

Columbus knew no more than the crew why the compass was behaving in this way. But he was the Captain, and it was necessary that he should reassure his men. He told them that the fault was not in the compass, but in the north star which moved from time to time. Fortunately the men believed him. If Columbus himself was worried, as he must have been, he was careful not to show it.

We know to-day that the magnetic north, to which a compass points, is not the true north, and its direction varies from different places on the earth's surface. Columbus did not know this.

The sailors were satisfied for the moment. But they continued to express their fears amongst themselves until some of them were ready to mutiny. They wanted to throw Columbus overboard and sail back to Spain.

All were, of course, looking for land to the westward, because a handsome reward had been promised to the man who first saw it. Then, one evening, one of the sailors called out that he had sighted land.

Columbus fell on his knees and returned thanks to God, and all on board the three ships sang a hymn of praise. All night they waited anxiously for the dawn, but when the morning came, the land was not there. What the sailor had seen was a low-lying cloud.

This disappointment made the sailors the more anxious to return to Spain, but fortunately that day a number of birds were seen. The men were again heartened, because Columbus assured them that such birds never flew far away from land.

The sea continued smooth, and again for a while the crews were content and hopeful.

This was on September the twenty-fifth, and though fortunately the sailors did not know it, they were to sail westwards for another eighteen days before they sighted land.

Columbus was ready to sail on, even if it took many months, but the crew had not his faith.

Another week passed, and another. Many more birds were seen, amongst them birds which seemed to be land birds. The crew no longer believed this to be a sign of land, and they went to Columbus complaining of the length of the voyage and demanding that the ships be put about. Columbus encouraged them as best he could, but they were again near to mutiny when fresh signs of land were seen to justify Columbus.

On October the eleventh the crew of the 'Pinta' found a carved log floating in the water, together with a branch loaded with what Columbus calls roseberries. Such things were better evidence of the nearness of land than birds, and that night the crews shared Columbus's excitement. They began to feel that the riches Columbus had promised them were within their grasp.

Their hopes were justified. At ten o'clock that night Columbus was standing on the poop of the 'Santa Maria' gazing to the west, as he had done day and night for five long weeks. Suddenly, far off in the distance, he saw a tiny spark of light.

It was too low to be a star. What was more, it moved as though someone were carrying a torch.

Columbus called to one of his officers who also saw the light, but by the time a third had been summoned, it had disappeared. Was it imagination, or some trick of the sea? Columbus could not be sure.

All night Columbus remained on the poop. The ships had shortened sail so that, if land were really there, they should not run aground in the dark. Slowly the sky behind them lightened, but to the westward all was dark. More and more they strained their eyes. Half the crew was up the rigging, the other half lining the bulwarks.

Then from a sailor high up at the mast-head of the 'Niña' came the cry, "Land ho!"

It was land at last! The long weeks, with nothing but sea all about them, were over. Many of the sailors thought they would never see land again, and all except Columbus were anxious and afraid. We can imagine how relieved they were at the sight of green trees on the horizon.

We must remember that the men who sailed with Columbus had never before been out of sight of land for more than a few hours, or days at most.

Columbus had believed that by sailing west he would reach India, the land route to which was closed by the Turks. He thought that the islands which he had found were somewhere near India, and the reason why they are still called the West Indies is owing to the mistake made by Columbus, almost five hundred years ago.

He landed with due formality, richly dressed and carrying the Spanish flag. With him were the two brothers Pinzon and many of the sailors. Once on shore Columbus knelt and kissed the ground with tears of joy. After giving thanks to God, he took possession of the island in the name of the King and Queen of Spain.

Columbus and his followers found themselves on a large, level island, with forest
trees growing round the rim of a blue bay.
On all sides were brilliantly coloured flowers
such as none of them had ever seen before.
After five weeks at sea, it was a paradise.

The natives showed no signs of fear.
Their skins were neither white nor black,
and their faces were painted in strange
patterns. They carried darts made of reeds,
tipped with sharks' teeth. It was clear that
they had never seen white men before, and
they had had no contact with the western
civilisation: When Columbus presented
them with strings of beads they were as
delighted as children with a new toy.

The Spaniards had seen natives before, on
the coast of Africa, but they were now to see
something new to them. The men of this
unknown island were holding little rolls of
brown leaves to which they applied fire,
drawing-off the smoke with their lips and
blowing it into the air. It was the white
man's first contact with tobacco.

One of the objects of the voyage was to discover the fabled golden islands where, it was believed, there were mountains of solid gold.

Some of the natives on San Salvador were wearing small gold ornaments, and Columbus questioned them as well as he could as to where the gold came from. They pointed to the south, and indicated that it came from a large island which they called Cuba. Columbus weighed anchor and sailed in search of it.

He imagined that it must be Japan. For more than two months he sailed from one island to another, landing on many of them and claiming them for Spain. He did not find either Japan or the island of gold. Instead, he met with a disaster which nearly wrecked the whole enterprise.

The 'Santa Maria' ran aground, owing to the carelessness of the steersman, on an island which Columbus named San Domingo. Soon the ship was a total wreck and Columbus was obliged to transfer himself and such stores as could be saved, to the 'Niña'. Leaving a garrison of forty men in a fort which he built on the shore, Columbus sailed for Spain.

After an adventurous voyage, the 'Niña' sailed into the harbour of Palos, eight months after leaving it. Soon the harbour was crowded with people who had never expected to see either Columbus or the ship again.

Columbus did not remain long in Palos. The King and Queen were at Barcelona, and Columbus hurried across Spain with the trophies he had brought back with him.

He made a triumphal entry into Barcelona followed by the crew carrying the parrots and other strange birds and beasts, as well as the ornaments and weapons of the natives of the newly discovered islands. But what most took the attention of the crowds were the natives themselves, half-a-dozen of whom Columbus had brought to Spain to be baptized as Christians.

Columbus was now the hero of the hour. At the Court where he had first been mocked and scorned by the courtiers, he was received with honour and seated at the right hand of the King. He was made an admiral of Spain and raised to the rank of a nobleman.

As he sat there in his great hour of triumph, Columbus must have felt that his patience, his determination, and his toil had been at last rewarded.

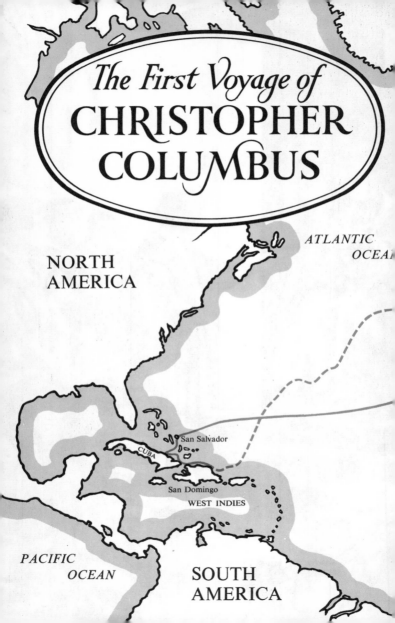

The First Voyage of
CHRISTOPHER
COLUMBUS

NORTH AMERICA

ATLANTIC OCEAN

San Salvador

CUBA

San Domingo

WEST INDIES

PACIFIC OCEAN

SOUTH AMERICA